For Lynn Rowland with many thanks – SG
For Tiziana – JB-B

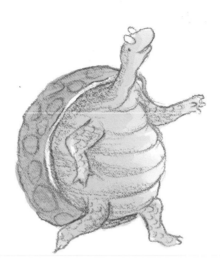

First published in Great Britain in 1999 by Bloomsbury Publishing Plc
38 Soho Square, London, W1V 5DF
This paperback edition first published 2000

Text copyright © Sally Grindley 1999
Illustrations copyright © John Bendall-Brunello 1999
The moral right of the author and illustrator has been asserted

A CIP catalogue record of this book is available from the British Library
ISBN 0 7475 4664 9 (paperback)
ISBN 0 7475 3650 3 (hardback)

Designed by Dawn Apperley

Printed in Singapore by Tien Wah Press

3 5 7 9 10 8 6 4

P₁ -3

AESOP'S FABLES

The Hare
and the
Tortoise
And Other Animal Stories

Sally Grindley and John Bendall-Brunello

BLOOMSBURY
CHILDREN'S
BOOKS

INTRODUCTION

Aesop has become a household name – most obviously for his fables, but also for the expressions that we use every day: 'sour grapes', 'a wolf in sheep's clothing', 'the boy who cried wolf', 'don't count your chickens before they are hatched', which almost certainly spring from his original fables. It is ironic therefore that we know so little about somebody who has had such an influence over the centuries. We think that he was Greek, and lived in the Sixth century BC. We think that he was probably a slave. Some say that he was thrown off a cliff at Delphi because of his stories, others that he was deformed in some way. And others say that he never existed at all...

Whatever the truth is, there can be no doubt that these stories of cunning and wit, of morality and lessons of character have enormous appeal. And in this younger picture book format we hope to broaden the audience for Aesop (whoever he was) and his fables. Sally Grindley's re-tellings race along with humour and verve, perfectly complemented by John Bendall-Brunello's lively illustrations. A book that we hope will be treasured, read and re-read for generations to come.

CONTENTS

The Hare and the Tortoise

One hot, sunny day, a hare was lazing on a grassy bank when he saw a tortoise walking slowly by. The hare snickered, then he sniggered, then he snorted, then he couldn't help himself and burst out laughing – '*TEE-HEE-HEE! HA-HA-HA!*'

The tortoise stopped and gazed at the hare. 'What's so funny?' she asked. 'It's your feet,' said the hare. 'They're so short – *TEE-HEE-HEE!* And you're so slow – *HA-HA-HA!* Do you ever arrive where you're going?'

The tortoise blinked thoughtfully and said, 'I may be slow, but I will beat you in a race.'

The hare couldn't believe his great big ears and burst out laughing again. 'What are you going to do, grow wings?' he giggled. 'All right, we'll meet here tomorrow morning. Make sure you eat your spinach – *HA-HA-HA!*'

With that, the hare leapt away to show how fast he was while the tortoise plodded on her way.

Bright and early the next morning, the hare and the tortoise lined up to begin their race. *READY, STEADY, GO!*

The hare shot off – *WHOOSH!* – and was quickly out of sight.

The tortoise set off at her usual pace – *PLOD, PLOD, PLOD.* She didn't stop to eat, she didn't stop to drink, she didn't stop to rest, she kept on going – *PLOD, PLOD, PLOD.*

The hare stopped to eat. The hare stopped to drink. The hare stopped to rest. 'Plenty of time,' he said. '*HA-HA-HA!* A tortoise can't beat a hare!' – and he soon fell fast asleep.

PLOD, PLOD, PLOD – the tortoise was closing the gap. *SNORE! SNORE!* – the tortoise was passing the hare. *PLOD, PLOD, PLOD* – the tortoise could see the finishing line.

The hare woke up and looked back down the path. 'Plenty of time,' he said. '*TEE-HEE-HEE!* She must be miles behind!'

But who was that in front of him? Whose short feet were crossing the finishing line?

'Wait!' yelled the hare. 'Too late,' said the tortoise, and she plodded on her way.

The Fox and the Grapes

Once upon a time, a very hungry fox was looking for food, when he saw the most enormous bunch of fat grapes hanging from a trellis.

O, how his eyes grew as big as saucers! O, how his tummy rumbled and his mouth watered!

'I must have those grapes,' panted the fox.

He leapt as high as he could, but he couldn't reach even the lowest hanging grape.

He stood on his hind legs on a wall, but the grapes dangled tantalisingly just above his nose, close enough to sniff but not close enough to bite.

'I'll get those grapes if it's the last thing I do,' he snapped.

He tried climbing up the trellis, but a rose tree grew there as well as the vine. 'Ow, ow, ow!' he yelped as he trod on one thorn after another. He jumped onto the grass and licked his wounds.

The fox couldn't believe his bad luck. He looked at the grapes one last time, then sloped away. 'I bet they tasted horrible, anyway,' he declared.

Then the fox grabbed a stick in his mouth and tried knocking the grapes down. Two of them came free. They fell to the ground. He leapt after them and tried to catch them, just as they rolled down a drain.

The Hare and the Hound

A hound was bounding across a field
one day when he startled a hare lazing
in the sun. The hare raced away, yelping
with fear – 'YELP, YELP, HELP!'
The hound chased after her snapping at
her heels and barking excitedly – 'WOOF,
WOOF, FOOD!' They ran this way and
that, dashing here, darting there. But
after a while the hound gave up the
chase and sat and washed his paws.

A young boy, seeing him stop, laughed at
him and said, 'That little hare is obviously
a much better runner than you.'

The hound stopped washing and
looked scornfully at the boy.

'You obviously haven't noticed an
important difference between us:
I was only running for my dinner.
She was running for her life.'

The Lion and the Mouse

One hot summer's day, a mouse stepped lightly across a lion's nose, thinking it was an unusually soft piece of ground.

The lion's paw stopped the mouse in her tracks and pinned her down by the tail. 'You woke me up, and now I'm hungry,' roared the lion, licking his lips and flexing his claws.

The mouse was terrified. 'Please let me go,' she squealed. 'I promise to help you if ever you are in trouble.'

The lion looked at the mouse and laughed his head off. 'Do you really think that you, a mere mouse, could ever help me, king of all beasts?' He laughed again, and was so amused at the idea of a mouse helping him that he let her go.

Some weeks later, the lion was caught in a trap set by hunters. A net made of strong rope fell over his head and was pulled tight round him. The lion roared a mighty roar – R - O - A - R! – and struggled to free himself. But the more he struggled, the more tied up in the net he became. R - O - A - R! he roared, angrily.

The mouse heard the lion roar. She remembered her promise and ran to find him. When she saw how he was caught, she began to gnaw at the rope with her sharp teeth.

'You'll never do it,' growled the lion. 'A little thing like you.'

'You'll be surprised,' said the mouse.

She went on gnawing, hour after hour, not stopping to rest, until at last she had made a hole big enough for the lion to crawl out.

'Never judge a thing by its size,' said the mouse, and she scampered away, leaving the lion lost for words.

The Fox and the Crow

Early one morning a crow plucked a big, fat, juicy worm from the ground and flew up into a tree with it. A passing fox saw her and determined to have the worm for breakfast. He quickly thought up a plan while the crow perched on a branch wondering which end of the worm to eat first.

'What a handsome bird is the crow!' declared the fox, loudly.

The crow, hearing the fox's words, fluttered her wings modestly.

'Her shape is so beautiful and her colouring magnificent!' continued the fox. The crow stretched her neck and proudly stuck out her chest.

'Oh, if only her voice were just as beautiful then she would deserve to be crowned Queen of the Birds!' said the fox, craftily.

The crow was annoyed that the fox didn't value her voice. 'CAW, CAW, CAW!' she cawed. 'There's nothing wrong with my –' As she opened her beak, the worm dropped straight into the fox's open mouth.

'My good crow,' said the fox, smugly, when he had swallowed the worm, 'there's nothing wrong with your voice, but there's plenty wrong with your brain.'

The Ants and the Grasshopper

All summer long the ants were busy. They built their nests, they laid their eggs, they cut up leaves and picked up crumbs, and they collected grain to put in their food store for the long winter days ahead – work, work, work, work, work.

And all summer long a grasshopper sat in the grass, watching the working ants, and singing loudly. He sang quick songs and slow songs, noisy songs and quiet songs, funny songs and sad songs – sing, sing, sing, sing, sing.

When autumn came, the ants busily dried out grain they had collected during the summer. Backwards and forwards they scurried, carrying pieces of grain to and from their nest.

Then winter came. The grasshopper, weak with hunger, crawled up to the ants and begged, 'Spare a little food for a poor, starving creature.'

The ants stopped in their tracks and asked, 'Why didn't you store food for yourself in the summer?'

The grasshopper replied, 'Oh, I was far too busy singing.'

The ants couldn't believe their ears. They laughed at him scornfully and said, 'If you were foolish enough to sing all summer, then you must dance to bed with an empty belly in the winter.'

With that they bade him good day and scuttled back to work.

The Jackdaw and the Doves

One winter's day, a hungry jackdaw watched
a family of doves pecking happily at some
seed the farmer had put out for them.
'Cor!' he squawked. 'I want some
of that!' Luckily for him, a pot of
white paint had been left in the
garden with the lid off. He flew
down to it, dipped in a wing, and
painted himself white all over.

Then he flew over to the doves and
mingled with them. As long as he was silent,
the doves thought he was one of them and he was
able to eat as much as he wanted.

But one day the jackdaw forgot himself and began to chatter. 'Lovely grub this, isn't it?' he said. 'Cor, you don't know how lucky you are to have humans feeding you every day.' The doves looked at him in horror. 'Imposter!' they shrilled. 'You're not one of us!' They pecked at him with their beaks and drove him away.

Smoothing his ruffled feathers, the jackdaw flew back to his own family and friends. 'I'm back,' he squawked. 'Have you missed me?' They took one look at him and screeched, 'Intruder! You're not one of us. Get away from here.' They too pecked at him with their beaks and drove him away.

The poor jackdaw had to live all on his own until he had grown new feathers and could be himself again.

The Mice in Council

One evening, a large family of mice gathered together for a meeting under the floorboards of a house.

'We have called this meeting,' announced one mouse, 'to find a way to outsmart our enemy, the cat.'

'If only we knew when he was coming,' said another mouse, 'he might not catch so many of us.'

'Has anyone got any ideas?' asked the third mouse.

The mice all started talking at once and came up with one idea after another.

'I've got a good idea,' squeaked one little mouse. 'We could tie a bell round his neck. When we hear it tinkling we'll know he's coming and can run away and hide.'

The other mice cheered loudly at this idea and patted the little mouse on the head.

'Well, then,' said the first mouse. 'There's only one last thing to be decided. Who is going to tie the bell round the cat's neck?'

The mice all looked at each other in horror. 'Tie the bell round the cat's neck! Not me!' they squeaked. 'Not me, not me, not me!'

The meeting closed with no agreement on any further action.

The Fox and the Goat

A fox was racing along one day when he fell down a well – WHOOPS! He tried and tried but he could not get out again.

A little while later, a very thirsty goat came to the same well. He looked down and saw the fox. 'What's the water like?' he bleated.

The fox put on a smiley face. 'It's the most delicious water I have ever tasted in my life. Come and try some.'

The goat didn't need to be told twice. He leapt straight in and gulped down as much water as he could until his thirst was quenched.

'The only problem is,' said the fox, as the goat stood licking his lips, 'I think we might be stuck here.'

The goat looked round the well and up at the steep walls and began to bleat miserably.

'I have a very clever plan, though,' said the fox, 'to help us both escape.'

The goat listened eagerly. He didn't want to be stuck down the well forever.

The fox continued. 'If you stretch your front legs up the side of the well as far as they will go and bend your head down, I will run up your back and leap out over the top. Then I will help you out.'

The goat agreed straightaway. He got himself into position, lowered his head, and stood quite still as the fox ran up his back, held on to his horns and hauled himself out of the well.

When the goat raised his head again, he saw the fox waving goodbye.

'Hey!' he bleated. 'Where are you going? You promised to help me out.'

The fox leaned over the wall and said, 'You are a foolish fellow. If you had as many brains in your head as you have hairs in your beard, you would never have jumped into the well in the first place without checking how you were going to get out. I am afraid I cannot help you.'

With that, the fox skipped away and left the goat to his fate.

The Peacock and the Crane

A peacock strutted into a garden and opened his
tail as wide as he could. Then he moved to a
spot where the light would shine right on
him, and stood there in all his splendour
thinking how wonderful he must look.
When a crane passed by, the peacock
looked at him and sneered. 'Where
were you when the colours were
given out? Here am I, dressed like
a king in gold and purple and all
the colours of the rainbow, and
there you are clothed from head
to toe in nothing but drab.'

The crane listened, then replied. 'There is some truth in what you say, but think on this: I can soar to the heights of heaven and lift up my voice to the stars, while you scratch below, just like a cock, among the birds of the dunghill.' With that, he rose into the air, hovered mockingly over the peacock's wilting tail, then flew away until he was just a dot on the horizon.

The Town Mouse and the Country Mouse

Late one autumn, a country mouse wrote to his close friend, a town mouse, and invited him for a meal. The town mouse was delighted to accept, and as he scuttled along the highways and byways he thought about the delicious food he would soon be enjoying.

As soon as he arrived, the country mouse eagerly led him out to the bare fields.

'Just look at all these scrumptious wheat stalks the farmer has left behind,' said the country mouse. 'If we dig around in the hedgerows there are the most juicy roots to be found. I'm so glad to be able to share such a wonderful meal with you, my friend.' With that he began to munch away happily. 'Mmmm,' he said. 'Yummy.'

The town mouse shivered in the cold autumn wind, trod gingerly over the muddy ground, and nibbled on a stalk. 'Ugh,' he muttered. 'It's so hard and scratchy.' He dug up a root. 'Yuck,' he mumbled. 'It's covered in dirt and the slugs have been at it.'

Before very long, he turned to the country mouse and said, 'I don't wish to be rude, my friend, but a fine fellow like you deserves an even better meal than this. Leave this for the ants and come with me to my house in town. There you shall eat like a king, and in warmth and comfort.'

The country mouse accepted straightaway and they scuttled along the highways and byways back to town. As soon as they arrived, the town mouse led his friend into a big room with a warm fire burning in a grate and a table piled high with bread and raisins and honey and nuts and strawberries and apples and grapes and the most enormous piece of holey cheese.

The country mouse could hardly believe his eyes. 'Wow!' he said. 'This really is a meal fit for a king, and it's so warm and the ground is smooth and clean. I feel quite ashamed when I think of the scratchy stalks and dirty roots I offered you.'

'Never mind,' said the town mouse. 'Let's eat.'

Just at that moment a door opened and heavy footsteps came across the floor. 'Quick!' squealed the town mouse. 'Jump down and hide!'

The two mice leapt from the table and ran as fast as they could to a hole in the wall, where they squeezed together, hearts pounding with fear.

They stayed there until the room was quiet again and then they climbed back onto the table. 'Better luck this time,' said the town mouse.

The country mouse picked up a fat juicy grape and was about to bite into it when he saw a big black nose resting on the table. Behind the nose two little black eyes were watching him hungrily. 'Help!' he squealed. 'WOOF, WOOF, WOOF!' barked the dog. The two mice leapt from the table and ran as fast as they could to the hole in the wall, where they squeezed together again, their fur stiff with fear.

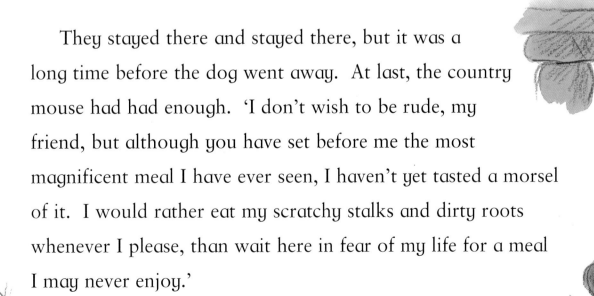

They stayed there and stayed there, but it was a long time before the dog went away. At last, the country mouse had had enough. 'I don't wish to be rude, my friend, but although you have set before me the most magnificent meal I have ever seen, I haven't yet tasted a morsel of it. I would rather eat my scratchy stalks and dirty roots whenever I please, than wait here in fear of my life for a meal I may never enjoy.'

The Wolf and the Goat

A wolf was searching for food on the lower slopes of a mountain, when he looked up and saw a goat feeding right on the edge of a steep precipice.

'Oh, my dear lady,' he cried. 'I beg you, do please be careful up there. I couldn't bear to see you fall. In fact, why don't you come and feed down here out of danger. The grass by my feet is as sweet as you will find anywhere.'

The goat looked down at the wolf and replied, politely: 'I think I'd prefer to stay here. I feel sure it is not my stomach you are anxious to fill, but your own.'

34

The Cockerel and the Jewel

Once upon a time, a hard-working cockerel spent all day scratching round the farmyard for something to eat for himself and his hens. 'Not a scrap, not a crumb, not a grain can I find for my poor hungry wives and my own starving self,' he grumbled.

Suddenly, he felt something hard under his foot. He scraped and scratched and scraped again, and uncovered a beautiful precious stone. 'Hmm,' he snorted, 'if your owner had found you he would have been over the moon with joy. As for me, I would rather have dug up one tiny grain of corn than all the lost jewels in the world. At least I could eat the corn!'

The Eagle and the Jackdaw

One fine morning an eagle sat on his nest high up on a cliff top and looked at the sheep grazing in the fields below. Suddenly, he swooped down, seized a young lamb in his giant talons and carried him effortlessly back up to his nest. A jackdaw watched the eagle from the roof of a barn and felt very envious.

'I can do that,' he said to himself. 'My feet might be smaller but I am just as strong, and I can fly as well as any bird if I put my mind to it.'

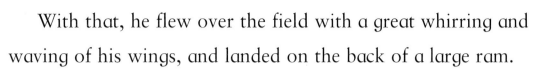

With that, he flew over the field with a great whirring and waving of his wings, and landed on the back of a large ram.

'Up we go!' he squawked. 'Up, up and away!'

He heaved with all his might, but he couldn't move the ram. He fluttered with his feathers and plucked with his claws, but the more he fluttered and plucked the more his claws became entangled in the ram's woolly coat.

'I'm stuck!' he squawked.

'Serves you right,' said the ram.

The shepherd saw what had happened and cut the jackdaw free. 'A daft bird you are,' he said. 'I'll clip your wings, that will stop your fancy ideas.'

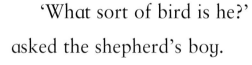

'What sort of bird is he?' asked the shepherd's boy.

'I know for sure he's a jackdaw,' said the shepherd, 'but he seems to think he's an eagle.'

The Bear and the Two Travellers

Two great friends were travelling along a dusty road together, when a bear jumped out onto the path right in front of them.

'I don't like the look of him,' said one friend. 'I'm out of here.' He quickly shinned up a tree and hid himself out of the bear's reach.

The other friend was left on his own, face to face with the bear, too frightened to move. The bear snarled – RRRRR! and the boy trembled – OOOOH! The bear growled – GRRR! and the boy shuddered – AAAH! The bear stood on his hind legs ready to attack. At once, the boy threw himself to the ground, held his breath and pretended to be dead.

The bear dropped down and ambled towards the boy. The boy kept as
still as he could. The bear smelt him all over and felt him with his snout.
He sniffed round his face and ears (that tickled and the boy nearly sneezed),
then he plodded away.

When he was sure the bear had
gone, the first boy climbed down
from his tree and jokingly said to
his friend, 'Hey, mate, what did
that grizzly whisper in your ear?'

The other boy replied, 'He
gave me some very good advice –
never travel with a friend who
runs away and leaves you at the
first sniff of danger.'

The Dog and the Shadow

One hot summer's day, a hungry dog snatched a piece of meat from
a farmer's table and hot-footed it home with the meat in his mouth.

On the way, he crossed a bridge over a stream and stopped to rest.
He looked down into the water and shook his head in disbelief. In the
water was another dog, bigger than him, with a piece of meat in his mouth
twice as big as his own.

'WOOF!' barked the dog on the bridge. 'I'll have that meat as well.'

He dropped his own piece of meat, leapt into the water and attacked the other dog fiercely. 'Fight me, come on, fight me!'

Spray flew everywhere as the dog hurled himself at the other dog. When at last he stopped, exhausted, and the water became calm, he finally saw the truth. There was no other dog and no other piece of meat. His own piece of meat was so far downstream he had lost it for ever.

'That will teach me to be greedy,' he whimpered.

The Shepherd Boy and the Wolf

There was once a shepherd boy whose job it was to look after a flock of sheep just outside a village.

One day, because he was bored, the shepherd boy screamed at the top of his voice, 'WOLF! WOLF! Help me, please, a wolf is attacking the sheep!'

People from the village ran to help as fast as they could, but when they reached the field all they found was the shepherd boy bursting his sides with laughter.

The shepherd boy was so pleased with the way he had fooled the villagers that he played the same trick three more times. Each time, the villagers came running. Each time the shepherd boy laughed until he ached.

Then, one day, a wolf really did break into the field. The shepherd boy was terrified. 'WOLF! WOLF! Help me, please, a wolf is attacking the sheep!'

Nobody listened.

'WOLF! WOLF! Help me, please, the wolf is killing the sheep!'

Nobody came.

The wolf, with no-one to stop him, soon destroyed the whole flock.

The shepherd boy, with no-one to turn to, burst into tears.

The Gnat and the Bull

One hot and humid day, a gnat settled down to rest on the horn of a bull. He stayed there for several hours stretching his tired legs, flapping his wings to keep cool and shifting from one position to another to make himself comfortable.

Finally he thought to himself, 'I'm growing bored.
Time to find another perch.' But before he flew away,
he buzzed loudly – BZZZZZ – hovered round the bull's
nose – BZZZZZ, and said, 'Thank you kindly for
allowing me to rest for so long on your splendid horn.
Will you mind terribly much if I go away now?' The
bull snorted loudly and replied, 'I hadn't the slightest
idea you had come, so why should I care two hoots if
you go?'

Acclaim for this book

' ... The child-friendly illustrations by John Bendall-Brunello
make it a lovely edition for the very young.' *The Children's Bookseller*

'These bite-sized pieces retell the best known and loved fables in an
easy to follow manner, perfect for introducing the stories of
wily animals and subtle morals to the young.' *Kids Out*